EXPLORATION & DISCOVERY

From AD1450 to AD1750

Dr Anne Millard

Illustrated by Joseph McEwan

Designed by Graham Round
Edited by Robyn Gee
Series editor Jenny Tyler

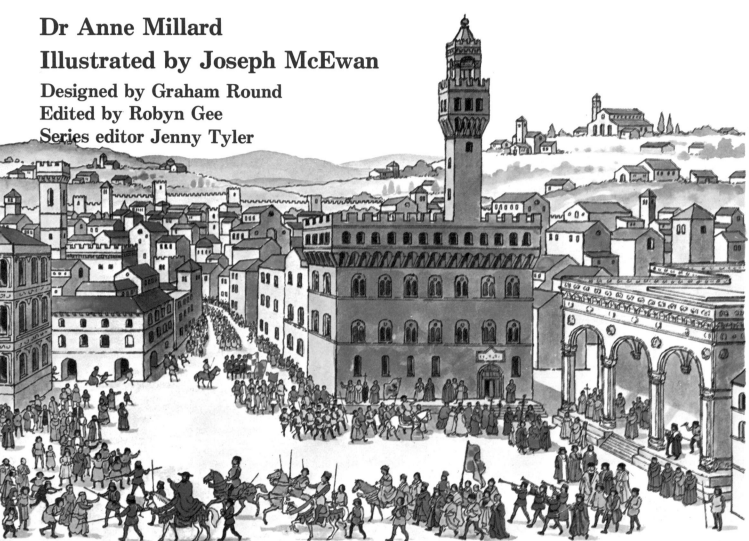

Contents

Consultant Editors: Brian Adams, Verulamium Museum, St Albans, England; D. Barrass, University of East Anglia, England; Ben Burt, Museum of Mankind, London, England; Elizabeth Carter, Institute of Archaeology, London, England; Dr M. C. Chapman, University of Hull, England; T. R. Clayton, University of Cambridge, England; Dr M. Falkus, London School of Economics, England; Dr C. J. Heywood, University of London, England; Dr Michael Loewe, University of Cambridge, England; Dr J. A. Sharpe, University of York, England; Dr C. D. Sheldon, University of Cambridge, England; R. W. Skelton, Victoria & Albert Museum, London, England; Dr R. Waller, University of Cambridge, England.
First published in 1979 by Usborne Publishing Ltd, 83-85 Saffron Hill, London EC1N 8RT.

Art and Learning

This book is about a time in the history of man when great changes were taking place. At the end of the 15th century,† people in Europe began to take a great interest in art and learning, and to develop new ideas about the world. They started asking questions and doing experiments, instead of just accepting existing ideas.

People began to think that civilisation had been at its best in Ancient Greece and Rome, so they revived Greek and Roman ideas. The time became known as the "Renaissance", which means revival or rebirth. It began in Italy and spread out through the rest of Europe.

The ideas of the Renaissance led on to other great changes in Europe. Traditional ideas about religion were challenged, experiments and inventions led to new weapons and ways of fighting and men set off to explore the world and discover new lands.

From this time on, European ideas influenced people all over the world.

This is the city of Florence in Italy. The new ideas of the Renaissance began here and many of the most famous men of this time lived and worked in Florence.

1 Painting

Before the Renaissance, artists painted mainly religious scenes. Everything in their pictures looked flat and the people did not look very lifelike.

2

In the late 14th and early 15th centuries, painters began to try to make the people in their paintings look as much like living people as possible.

3

Besides painting religious subjects, Renaissance painters did pictures, like this one, of everyday life, and of stories from Ancient Greece and Rome.

Sculpture

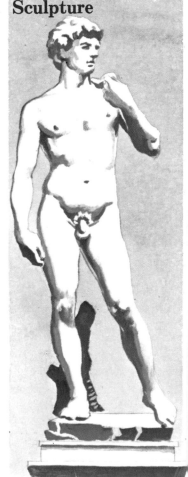

Sculptors were inspired by the statues of Ancient Greece and Rome. This marble statue was made by Michelangelo. He was also a painter, an architect and a poet.

4

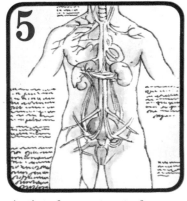

For the first time artists began to use live models to help them paint life-like people. This is Simonetta Vespucci, who modelled for the artist Botticelli.

5

Artists began to study nature and the human body to help them draw things more accurately. This sketch is from the notebook of Leonardo da Vinci.

6

Artists learned how to show distance in their paintings, making you feel you could walk into them. This is called "perspective".

1 Learning

Many new universities and schools were founded. The main subjects were Greek and Latin grammar. In England the new schools were called "grammar" schools.

2

Scholars studied texts in Greek, Latin and Hebrew. They were excited by the thoughts and ideas of ancient times. The invention of printing helped to spread these ideas.

3

Studying ancient Christian texts made some people, like this Dutch scholar called Erasmus, criticize the Church and its priests for being corrupt.

4

People also began to study politics. This is Machiavelli, an Italian who wrote a book about politics called "The Prince", in which he said that a ruler had to be ruthless.

Architecture

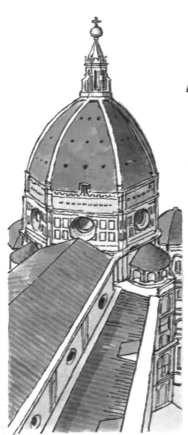

Architects built wonderful palaces and churches. They used domes and copied the style of Greek and Roman temples. The towers and spires of the Middle Ages went out of fashion.

A properly educated Renaissance person was expected to be able to:

understand and collect art,

write poetry,

play a musical instrument,

read and write Latin and Greek,

speak several languages,

fight if necessary,

take part in politics,

ride and be good at sports,

show good manners to everyone.

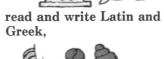

†This means the 100 years between AD1400 and AD1500.

Science and Inventions

1

The new ideas of the Renaissance made people keen to question everything about the world around them. Some people began doing experiments to test their ideas.

2

People called "alchemists", however, tried to brew potions that would cure all ills, give eternal life and turn lead into gold.

3

One of the greatest men of the Renaissance was Leonardo da Vinci. He was a painter and an inventor and he thought a lot about making a flying machine. This is a model based on one of his designs which he worked out by watching birds fly. Leonardo also studied animals and human bodies to find out how they worked and he painted the very famous picture of the Mona Lisa.

4

The printing press was probably the most important invention of this time. The first one was made by a German called Johann Gutenberg. Books could now be produced quickly and cheaply, instead of having to be handwritten as before. This meant ideas and learning spread more quickly.

5

In England, people experimented with metals and learnt how to make cheap and reliable cannons out of cast-iron. These soon replaced the expensive bronze cannons that the Germans and Italians had been making.

6

There were very few clocks in the Middle Ages and these were usually huge ones on public buildings. The invention of springs made it possible to make watches that could be carried around and also small clocks that people could keep at home. Pendulum clocks were also invented at this time.

7

During the 16th century, the invention and improvement of instruments like these helped sailors to steer their ships more accurately. To make the most of these instruments a captain had to know the stars and be good at mathematics. Gradually, new and better maps were produced too.

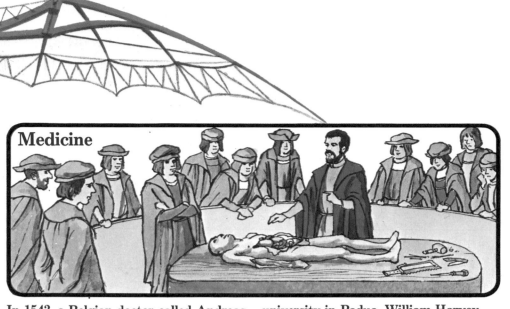

Medicine

In 1543, a Belgian doctor called Andreas Vesalius published a book about how the human body worked. Here he is lecturing to his students at the university in Padua. William Harvey, another great doctor, discovered and proved that the heart pumps blood round the body.

The invention of microscopes made people realize for the first time that the world was full of minute creatures, too small to see unless they are magnified.

1 Ideas about the universe

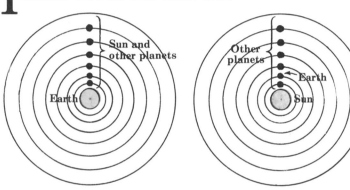

From the time of the Ancient Greeks onwards, people had believed that the Earth was the centre of the universe and that the Sun, Moon and stars moved round it. In 1543, the Polish astronomer, Copernicus, published a book showing that the Sun, not the Earth, was the centre of the universe. Many people refused to believe him.

The invention of the telescope in the early 17th century meant that people could get a better view of the stars and planets. The Italian scientist, Galileo, made a telescope strong enough to show the separate stars of the Milky Way. He supported Copernicus, but the Catholic Church forbade him to teach his theories.

The new interest in science led to the founding of scientific societies. Special places were built, like the Royal Observatory near London, for the study of stars.

This wall has been cut away.

The discoveries of the English scientist, Sir Isaac Newton, changed people's ideas about the universe. Here he is doing an experiment through which he discovered that white light is made up of different colours.

Key dates

AD1444/1510	Italian painter, **Botticelli**.
AD1452/1519	Italian artist/inventor **Leonardo da Vinci**.
AD1454	**Gutenberg** invented his printing press.
AD1466/1536	Dutch scholar **Erasmus**.
AD1469/1527	Italian writer **Machiavelli**.
AD1473/1543	Polish astronomer **Copernicus**.
AD1475/1564	Italian artist **Michelangelo**.
AD1514/1564	Belgian doctor **Vesalius**.
AD1564/1642	Italian astronomer **Galileo**.
AD1578/1657	English doctor **Harvey**.
AD1600 (approx.)	Invention of telescope and microscope.
AD1642/1727	English scientist **Newton**.

New Ideas About Religion

The people of Western Europe were all Roman Catholics, but by AD1500, many were unhappy with the way the Church was being run. The Popes and many of the priests seemed interested only in wealth and power and set a bad example in the way they lived their lives. This led to a movement, which became known as the "Reformation", to change and reform the Christian Church. People who joined the movement were called "Protestants" because they were protesting about things that they thought were wrong.

In 1517 a German monk called Martin Luther nailed a list of 95 complaints about the Church and the way priests behaved, to the door of Wittenberg church in Germany.

Luther believed that everyone should be able to study God's message for themselves. So he translated the Bible from Latin into German. Versions in other languages quickly followed.

The Catholics fight back

The Pope called a meeting of churchmen at Trent in Italy. They laid down exactly what the beliefs and rules of the Catholic Church were and ordered complete obedience to them.

This is St Ignatius Loyola who founded the Society of Jesus. The members, who were known as Jesuits, tried to win Protestants back to the Catholic Church.

Many Protestants disapproved of decorated churches and destroyed those they took over. But the Catholics introduced an even more elaborate style, shown here, called Baroque.

Murders and executions

Holland was ruled by the Kings of Spain at this time. William of Orange led a revolt of the Dutch Protestants against the Spanish. He was murdered by a Catholic.

So many people in France became Protestants that the Catholics laid a plot. On 24 August 1572, the eve of St Bartholomew's Day, they murdered all the Protestants they could find in Paris.

Mary, Queen of Scots, was a Catholic. She plotted against Elizabeth I, the Protestant Queen of England, and was taken prisoner by the English. She was executed at Fotheringay Castle.

Luther was condemned by a Church court, but several German princes supported him. He also won followers across Europe.

King Henry VIII of England wanted to divorce his wife and marry Anne Boleyn. The Pope would not let him, so Henry made himself head of the Church in England.

Soon there were other religious leaders and the Protestants split into different groups. This is John Calvin, who set up a new Church in Geneva.

Priests on both sides were tortured and even hanged. Both Protestants and Catholics believed they were saving their opponents from hell by doing this.

In Spain, the most fiercely Catholic country in Europe, there was an organization called the Inquisition, which hunted out anyone who was not a good Catholic. The officers of the Inquisition used torture to make people confess their beliefs. Protestants who refused to become Catholics were burnt to death at special ceremonies called "Auto-da-fe" (Spanish for "acts of faith"), which were watched by huge crowds.

This is a map of Europe in about AD1600. It shows which areas were still Catholic and which had become Protestant.

Protestant

Catholic

ENGLAND

GERMAN STATES

FRANCE

Mixture of Catholic and Protestant

PORTUGAL

SPAIN

ITALIAN STATES

War and Weapons

Guns were invented at the beginning of the 14th century. It was many years before they came into general use, but over the next few centuries they completely changed the way wars were fought. The knights and castles of the Middle Ages gradually disappeared. Their armour was no protection against bullets, so they could not get close enough to the enemy to use their swords and lances. Castle walls could not stand up to an attack of cannon balls.

From about 1300 onwards, archers started using longbows which were very effective against knights. They had a long range and were quite accurate.

Castles and walled towns had been very difficult to capture, but when cannons began to be used in the 15th century, even the thickest walls could be quickly battered down.

Armour and weapons were expensive. When peasants rebelled, as they often did in the 15th and 16th centuries, they had little chance against well-armed knights and nobles. This is a German knight charging a peasant.

When hand-guns were first invented they took a long time to load and were not very accurate. Pikemen were positioned next to the gunmen to protect them against charging cavalry while they reloaded.

Then guns called muskets were invented. They fired more accurately but at first they were too heavy to hold. The musketeers had to use forked sticks to support their guns.

Pistols were less accurate than muskets and fired a shorter distance. They were usually used by cavalry who rode at the enemy, fired at them and rode away to reload.

Towards the end of the 17th century soldiers started to use bayonets (blades which attach to the end of a gun). Gunmen could now defend themselves at close-quarters.

8 Instead of relying on their nobles to raise armies, or hiring mercenary soldiers, kings began to set up permanent armies of their own. These armies were much more highly-trained than before and could obey orders at speed. Commanders had to study hard to learn how to plan their battles and campaigns.

9 War at sea changed too. The Dutch and English developed lighter ships which could turn much more quickly. This helped the English fleet to defeat the Spanish Armada.

10 On ships, cannons were placed along each side. Enemies tried to fire "broadside" at each other so they would have more chance of hitting their target.

11 Disease, bad food and harsh punishments made life at sea very hard. Governments often used "press-gangs" to kidnap men for the navy and take them to sea by force.

Key dates

AD1455/1485 **Wars of the Roses**: civil war in England.

AD1494/1559 **Italian Wars**: Italian states fighting each other. France and the Holy Empire joined in.

AD1524/1525 **Peasants' War** in Germany: the German peasants rebelled.

AD1562/1598 **Wars of Religion in France**: fighting between French Catholics and Protestants.

AD1568/1609 **Dutch Revolt**: the Dutch rebelled against their Spanish rulers.

AD1588 The **Spanish Armada** was defeated by the English fleet.

AD1618/1648 **Thirty Years War**: fought mainly in Germany. Involved most of the countries of Europe.

AD1642/1649 **Civil War** in England.

AD1648/1653 **Wars of the "Fronde"**: two rebellions against the French government.

AD1652/1654, **Wars between the Dutch and**
1665/1667 & **the English.** Fought at sea.
1672/1674 Caused by rivalry over trade.

AD1701/1714 **War of the Spanish Succession**: France and Spain against England, Austria and Holland.

AD1733/1735 **War of the Polish Succession**: Austria and Russia against France and Spain about who should rule Poland.

AD1740/1748 **War of the Austrian Succession**: Austria, Britain and Russia against France and Prussia.

The Incas

The Incas lived in the mountains of Peru in South America. Their capital was a city called Cuzco. From about 1440 onwards they began to conquer neighbouring lands and build up a huge empire. The empire lasted about a hundred years before Spanish soldiers arrived in search of gold and conquered them.

White llamas to be sacrificed.

Temple

Atahualpa

Body of Huayna Capac

Musicians with drums, rattles and flutes.

The emperor of the Incas was called the Inca. His people thought he was descended from the Sun and when he died his body was preserved and treated with great honour.

This is the funeral procession of an emperor called Huayna Capac. His son, Atahualpa, became the new emperor by fighting his half-brother, Huascar.

Unfortunately this war, was just before the Spaniards arrived and it greatly weakened the Incas in their fight against the European invaders.

Inca priests were very important people. They held services, heard confessions and foretold the future by looking into the fire. The Sun was their chief god.

Women were taught how to weave and spin wool. Some women, who were specially chosen for their beauty, became priestesses called the Virgins of the Sun.

The Incas were very skilled at making things out of gold. This gold glove was found in a tomb. Beside it is a model of a god, set with precious stones.

A farming village

Land has been terraced so that crops can be grown on the steep mountainside.

Peasants dig fields with pointed sticks.

Buildings made with heavy blocks of stone have been put together without the help of machinery or iron tools.

Villagers eat mainly maize and vegetables.

Women weaving

Guinea pigs are kept for food.

Men drinking "chicha" beer

All the land belonged to the Inca. One third of the crops was kept by peasants, who lived in mountain villages, like this one, and worked on the land. Another third went to the priests and the last third went to the Inca. With his share he paid his officials, soldiers and craftsmen.

Keeping records

The Incas had no system of writing but their officials used "quipus" to help them record things. Coloured strings stood for objects. Knots tied in the strings stood for numbers.

Roads and messengers

A well-maintained network of roads linked all parts of the huge Inca empire. There were hanging bridges, made of twisted straw and vines, across the mountain chasms. These roads and bridges were built and repaired by peasants sent from their villages to serve the emperor. There were no wheeled vehicles so goods were carried by llamas and relays of fast runners carried messages and quipus across the empire. There were rest houses, a day's journey apart, for people on official business to stay in.

The Discovery of America

Until the end of the 15th century, Europeans did not know that the huge continent of America existed. Explorers and traders had made long and difficult journeys eastwards to China and India, bringing back spices, silks and jewels. These were in such demand in Europe that people thought there might be a quicker way to the Far East by sea. The Portuguese sailed to the east round Africa, but others thought it might be quicker to go westwards. When they did, they found America in the way.

1

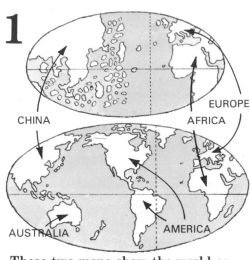

These two maps show the world as people in Europe thought it looked in about 1490 (top) and as it really looked (bottom).

An Italian, called Christopher Columbus, persuaded King Ferdinand and Queen Isabella of Spain to pay for an expedition to find China by sailing west instead of east. He set off in 1492 with three ships.

1 The Spanish conquerors

Spanish adventurers ("conquistadors") started to explore the mainland, hoping to find treasure. They discovered the Aztecs in Mexico and the Incas in Peru.

Spanish soldiers, led by Hernando Cortes, attacked the Aztecs in their capital city, Tenochtitlan. Although there were fewer of them, the Spaniards had much better weapons than the Indians, who had never seen horses before. The Spaniards soon conquered the whole of Mexico and called it New Spain.

With the help of his Indian interpreter, Dona Marina, Cortes won the support of several Indian tribes, who helped him to defeat the Aztecs.

In Peru, the Spanish, led by Pizarro, captured the Inca emperor. To buy his freedom he filled a room with gold. But he was killed and Peru conquered.

The Spanish tried to make all the Indians become Christians. Indians who went on worshipping their own gods were burnt to death.

The Spaniards treated the Indians very cruelly. Many were put to work in silver mines. Thousands died of illnesses brought over from Europe.

3 After five weeks, Columbus reached what he thought were islands off China but were, in fact, the West Indies. Later, he made three more voyages and reached the mainland of America.

4 To stop Spain and Portugal fighting about who owned the newly discovered lands, the Pope drew a line on the map. All new lands east of the line went to Portugal, those to the west went to Spain.

5 There were many expeditions to explore the new lands. The first to sail round South America was led by Magellan. He was killed on the way, but his ship returned and was the first to sail right round the world.

Slave trade

The Spanish and Portuguese brought ships full of Africans over to work as slaves. They tried to stop other countries joining in this trade, but some captains, like the Englishman John Hawkins, ignored their ban.

Pirates

AZTEC EMPIRE

INCA EMPIRE

Columbus's route

WEST INDIES

Pope's line

Magellan's route

Spanish treasure ships were often attacked by pirates on their way back to Spain. The French and English governments even encouraged their sea-captains to be pirates, rewarding them for bringing back treasure.

Key dates

AD1492	First voyage of **Christopher Columbus**.
AD1494	The Pope divided the new lands between Spain and Portugal.
AD1498	**Vasco da Gama** sailed round Africa and reached India.
AD1500	**Pedro Cabral** claimed Brazil for the Portuguese government.
AD1519/1522	**Magellan's** voyage round the world.
AD1519	**Hernando Cortes** landed in Mexico.
AD1521	Fall of Aztec capital, Tenochtitlan.
AD1533	Murder of the Inca, **Atahualpa**.
AD1562/1568	**John Hawkins** shipping African slaves to Spanish America.

Muslim Empires

From about 1300, a Muslim* people called the Ottoman Turks began to build up an empire. In 1453 they captured Constantinople, the centre of the Orthodox Christian Church, and renamed the city Istanbul. Its great cathedral, St Sophia, shown here, became a mosque.

The Ottomans wanted to conquer Europe. Led by Sultan, Suleiman the Magnificent, they defeated the Hungarian army at the Battle of Mohács, and took control of Hungary. They continued to threaten Europe until 1683, when they besieged Vienna and were heavily defeated.

The Sultan's palace

Slaves

This is a slave. The Ottomans chose boys from the Christian areas of their empire, took them away from their families and brought them up as Muslims.

Most of the boys were trained to be soldiers called Janissaries. They were the best troops in the Ottomans' army.

The cleverest of these boys were given a good education, and later they were made government officials.

The Ottoman Sultans spent much of their time in the Topkapi Saray, their splendid palace in Istanbul. Here the Sultan is receiving an envoy from Europe. European princes were eager to buy Turkish goods and make alliances with the Turks.

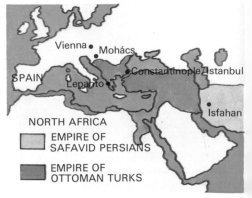

EMPIRE OF SAFAVID PERSIANS

EMPIRE OF OTTOMAN TURKS

*Muslims belong to a religion called Islam.

Muslims in Persia

1

The Persians, like the Ottomans, were Muslims, but they belonged to a different group of Muslims, called the Shi'ites. This mosque is in Isfahan, their capital city.

2

The Persians and Ottomans often fought each other over religion and land. Their wars lasted on and off for over 200 years.

3

The royal family of Persia was called the Safavids. During the reign of their greatest shah (king), Abbas I, the luxuries of Persia became famous throughout the world.

1 Spain and the Muslims

Muslims had overrun Spain in the 8th century. They were finally driven out when King Ferdinand and Queen Isabella conquered Granada, the last Muslim kingdom in Spain.

2

Some Muslims stayed on in Spain and became Christians. But the Spaniards never trusted them and years later their descendants were banished.

3

The Spanish wanted to keep the Ottomans out of the Mediterranean Sea. In 1571, they defeated them in the great Battle of Lepanto.

4

Fierce pirates from North Africa raided the coasts of Spain and other European countries and carried off people to sell as slaves in Muslim lands.

15

The Habsburgs

SPANISH HABSBURG LANDS AUSTRIAN HABSBURG LANDS

The Habsburgs were the most powerful ruling family in Europe in the 16th century. They were the rulers of Austria and most of Central Europe and in 1516 the Habsburg Archduke, Charles V, inherited Spain and the newly won Spanish territories in America too. When Charles died, his empire was divided between his son, Philip II of Spain, and his brother Ferdinand, Archduke of Austria, and from then on Spain and Austria were ruled by separate branches of the Habsburg family.

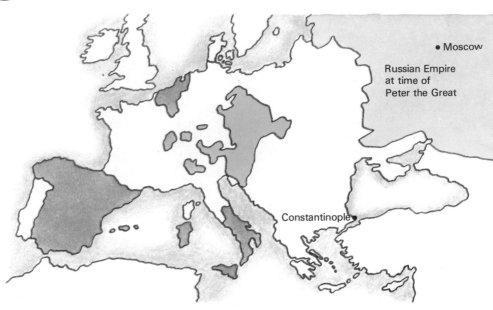

Moscow

Russian Empire at time of Peter the Great

Constantinople

1 Fabulous riches were sent to Spain from South America, but wars against the French, the Protestants and the Turks cost so much that the kings of Spain were always in debt.

2 You can see some of the magnificent clothes worn at the Spanish court in the paintings of Velasquez, King Philip IV's court artist. This is Philip's daughter, Margarita Teresa.

3 The Spanish kings were strong supporters of the Catholic Church. They encouraged the Inquisition to find and punish heretics and declared war on Protestant countries.

4 At this time there were many famous writers and artists in Spain. This is Don Quixote with his servant Sancho Panza, from the book *Don Quixote* written by Miguel de Cervantes.

Holy Roman Emperors

This is the Holy Roman Emperor, who was elected by a group of seven German princes. They always elected the Habsburg Archduke of Austria because the Habsburgs were so powerful. This meant that the Archduke ruled over the hundreds of different German states. This was a difficult task as many of the German princes had become Protestant and resented having a Catholic ruler.

The Tsars

Before 1450, Russia was divided into several different states, each with its own ruler. During the 15th century, the Grand Prince of Moscow gradually gained control of all the states. The Russians belonged to the Orthodox Christian Church, which had its centre at Constantinople. But when the Turks, who were Muslims, conquered Constantinople in 1453, Moscow saw itself as the centre of the Orthodox Church.

1

Grand Prince Ivan III of Moscow was the first to use the title "Tsar" and have this double-headed eagle as his emblem.

2

Ivan III ordered that Moscow's fortress, the Kremlin, should be rebuilt. He brought in Italian architects who built the cathedral, shown here, inside its walls.

3

Ivan IV (1533/1584), often known as Ivan the Terrible because of his cruelty, won great victories over the Tartars and also gained control of all the Russian nobles.

He encouraged trade with Europe and is here receiving envoys from Elizabeth I of England.

4

When Ivan the Terrible died, the nobles fought for power until a national assembly chose Michael Romanov, shown here, to be the Tsar.

Peter the Great

Tsar Peter the Great (1689-1725) wanted Russia to become a powerful modern state. He forced his nobles to become more European by making them cut their beards off.

Peter went to Holland and England to learn about ship-building. He brought European craftsmen back with him to build him a strong, new navy.

In 1709, Peter led the Russians to a great victory over Sweden, their main rival, at the Battle of Poltava.

Peter wanted Russia to have the grandest capital city in Europe, so he built St Petersburg (now Leningrad) on the edge of the Baltic Sea.

The Elizabethans

From 1485 to 1603, England was ruled by a family called the Tudors. The best-known of the Tudor rulers are Henry VIII, who separated the English Church from the Roman Catholic, and his daughter, Elizabeth I. When Elizabeth was only three, her mother, Anne Boleyn, was executed. During the reigns of her half-brother Edward VI and half-sister Mary, Elizabeth's life was often in danger, but she survived to become one of England's most brilliant rulers.

1 This is a painting of Elizabeth. She reigned for 45 years, keeping a magnificent court where she inspired writers, artists and explorers. She never married.

2 This is a Protestant preacher. Elizabeth declared that the Church of England was Protestant, but she did not persecute people who had other beliefs unless they plotted against her.

Explorers

This is Sir Walter Raleigh. He introduced tobacco and potatoes to England from America. He also tried to start a colony in America, but it was unsuccessful.

Some explorers tried to find a way to the Far East by sailing north-west or north-east. They all failed because their ships could not break through the ice.

Once the explorers had discovered new lands and sea-routes, merchants banded together to form companies to trade overseas, licensed by the government.

The Globe theatre

The more expensive seats are in the galleries.

Pit where poorer people and apprentices stand.

The theatre is built of wood with a thatched roof so there is always a danger of fire. (It did, in fact, burn down in 1613.)

Francis Drake

Francis Drake was a great sailor who led daring attacks on Spanish ships and colonies in South America and captured a lot of treasure from them. The Spaniards hated him, but after he had sailed round the world the queen had him knighted on his ship, the Golden Hind. Later, when the Spaniards sent an Armada (fleet) to invade England, Drake played a leading part in their defeat.

By avoiding expensive wars, Elizabeth helped England become very wealthy. The nobles and middle classes spent their money on splendid houses, furniture and clothes.

Beggars and thieves were a terrible problem. A new law was made which said that all districts must provide work for the poor and shelter those who could not work.

Portraits

We know what many famous Elizabethans looked like from the miniature portraits by an artist called Nicholas Hilliard. This is a picture he painted of himself.

Musicians

Several great musicians lived at this time. Two of the most famous were Thomas Tallis and William Byrd. They composed music to be played at home as well as a great deal of church music.

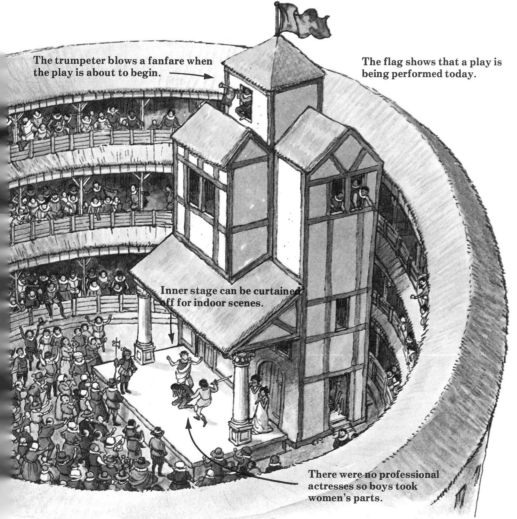

The trumpeter blows a fanfare when the play is about to begin.

The flag shows that a play is being performed today.

Inner stage can be curtained off for indoor scenes.

There were no professional actresses so boys took women's parts.

The Globe in London was the most famous of the theatres built at this time. The first one was opened in 1576. Before this, plays were performed in inn courtyards and town squares.

Shakespeare was an actor and writer with one of the London companies. He wrote at least 36 plays and many of them were first performed at the Globe theatre.

19

European Settlers

An Indian village

Land cleared by burning.

Boys fishing

Chief

Long houses made of bark.

Party of hunters bringing a deer home.

Palisade made of tree trunks.

Ritual dance

When the first Europeans arrived in North America, there were hundreds of different tribes of native people there. Each had their own customs, language and way of life. Those on the east coast, where the settlers first landed, were farmers, hunters and food gatherers. They lived in small villages and grew corn and some vegetables. This picture is based on drawings made by some of the early European settlers. The arrival of Europeans in the early 17th century was a disaster for these Indians. Many of them died of diseases brought from Europe and many others were killed or driven from their lands.

13 colonies

Mississippi River

The Appalachian Mountains

New England

Boston

Jamestown

Louisiana

In 1607 a group of English settlers set up a colony at Jamestown in Virginia. Here, their leader, Captain John Smith, is being rescued from death by Pocahontas, the daughter of the local Indian chief.

Another group of English people, who became known as the Pilgrim Fathers, sailed to America in 1620 in the ship, "Mayflower". They were Puritans, who wanted freedom to worship God in their own way.

3 The Puritans called the area where they settled New England. During their first winter they had a terrible struggle getting enough food.

4 Local Indians helped the English to survive. After their first harvest they held a feast to thank God. "Thanksgiving Day" is still celebrated in America.

5

Many other Europeans sailed with their families and belongings to live in America. Here is a ship full of settlers unloading. Some of them went because they wanted religious freedom, some were escaping from troubles at home and others came in the hope of finding adventure, or a better life and land of their own. The settlers on the east coast soon formed 13 colonies, each with their own laws and system of government. Gradually they were all brought under the control of the British government.

6 Most colonists settled down as farmers, at first. It was hard work clearing the land, growing crops and defending themselves against hostile Indians.

7 In the south the colonists started growing tobacco. There was a craze for it in Europe so they grew rich by making African slaves work for them.

8 Trade with Europe became profitable and some of the money was used to build towns. This is part of 18th century Boston.

9 A few people, mainly Frenchmen, chose to live as trappers and hunters. They explored along the Mississippi River, claiming land for France.

Plantations and Trading Forts

1 West Indies

Plantation owner

Sugar cane

Overseer

From the 1620s onwards, most of the islands known as the West Indies were taken over by the French and English. They set up sugar plantations and imported African slaves to work on them.

2

Fierce pirates infested the Caribbean Sea at this time. One English pirate called Henry Morgan was eventually knighted by King Charles II.

Key dates

AD1497	**John Cabot** discovered Newfoundland.
AD1523	French begin to explore Canada.
AD1607	English colony set up in Virginia.
AD1608	French founded the settlement of Quebec.
AD1612	First English colony in West Indies set up on Bermuda.
AD1620	The Pilgrim Fathers sailed to America in the Mayflower.
AD1655	English captured Jamaica from Spaniards.
AD1682	The French set up settlements in Louisiana.
AD1759	**General James Wolfe** captured Quebec from the French.
AD1763	Treaty of Paris. England took over Canada from French.

Canadian trading fort

Many French and English people settled in Canada. Some of them were farmers but many of them made a living by trapping animals for fur and catching and salting fish, especially cod. The trappers sold their catch and bought supplies at forts set up by trading companies. The fish and furs were then sent to Europe where they were in great demand.

BRITISH

SPANISH

FRENCH

Hudson's Bay Company

Quebec

CANADA

WEST INDIES

JAMAICA

CARIBBEAN SEA

The capture of Quebec

The lands belonging to England's Hudson Bay Company in Canada and the 13 colonies in America were separated by the French colonies in Canada. From the 1680s onwards, rivalry between the French and British grew and fighting broke out. Here British troops, led by general Wolfe, are reaching the top of the very steep cliffs above the St Lawrence River before making a surprise attack on the French city of Quebec. After the capture of Quebec, the English went on to gain control of the whole of Canada.

The Kingdom of Benin

1

Today Benin is a small town in Nigeria, but between AD1450 and AD1850 it was the capital city of a great kingdom. European explorers brought back reports that Benin's warriors were highly disciplined and very brave, and were constantly fighting to win more land and slaves.

2

The people of Benin had no system of writing, but they made bronze plaques to record important events. This plaque shows their king, who was called the Oba, sacrificing a cow. The Obas spent most of their time in religious ceremonies and let their counsellors govern.

3

The Portuguese were the first Europeans to explore the coast of Africa. Soon others came, eager to buy ivory, gold and especially slaves sold by the local chiefs.

4

The most promising boys were trained as hunters. If they were very good they could become elephant hunters, armed with blow-guns and poisonous darts.

5

Benin lost its power in the 19th century, but the people still survive. This present-day chief is dressed for a festival in honour of the Oba's father.

Music

This carving shows a drummer playing at a ceremony at the Oba's court. The musicians of Benin also played bells and elephant-tusk trumpets.

Carvings

The people of Benin made beautiful portrait heads, like this one of a queen mother. It was the queen mother's duty to bring up the Oba's heir.

There were many skilled craftsmen in Benin. Besides bronze plaques and portrait heads, they made lovely things from ivory, like the bracelets, shown above.

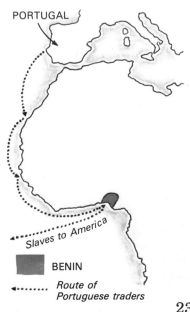

PORTUGAL

Slaves to America

◼ BENIN

.... *Route of Portuguese traders*

The Mogul Empire

Muslim warriors had been invading and setting up kingdoms in India since before the 10th century. The most famous Muslim invaders were the Moguls, who were descended from the Mongols. In 1526, they founded the great Mogul Empire in north-west India which lasted until 1858. During their rule, great progress was made in the arts and sciences. Most Indians continued to work on the land, however, as their ancestors had done for centuries before them.

This is the first Mogul emperor, Babur (1526-1530). He was a descendent of the Mongol chiefs, Tamerlane and Genghis Khan.

This is the court of Babur's grandson, Akbar (1556-1605), greatest of the Mogul emperors. He was a good soldier and a wise ruler. He encouraged artists and brought scholars of all religions together to try to find one religion.

The Moguls were strongly influenced by Persian art and learning. This is Akbar's son, whose wife was Persian. Her name, Nurjahan, meant "Light of the World".

Many wonderful buildings were put up by the Moguls. The most famous is the Taj Mahal. It was built by Emperor Shah Jahan, as a tomb for his wife Mumtaz Mahal.

The Mogul emperors and nobles enjoyed hunting. Sometimes they used cheetahs for hunting gazelle. They also hunted tigers while riding on the backs of elephants.

European merchants came to India to buy silks, cotton, ivory, dyes and spices. Gradually they set up trading posts throughout India.

As the power of the Mogul rulers grew weaker, the British and French used the rivalry of lesser princes to increase their own power. Here, one of the princes is preparing for battle.

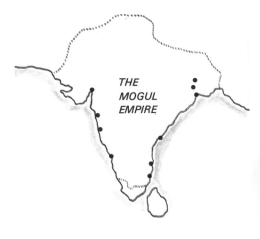

THE MOGUL EMPIRE

• BRITISH AND FRENCH TRADING POSTS

Ming and Ch'ing Emperors

The emperors of China lived in Peking, in a fantastic palace called the "Forbidden City". Here they were surrounded by richly decorated buildings and lovely gardens. The Ming dynasty (family line) of emperors (AD1368/1644) cut themselves off from the government and let their officials rule for them. In AD1644 the last Ming emperor committed suicide and the Ch'ing dynasty won power. They ruled until AD1911. Many of the Ch'ing emperors were clever rulers and brought peace and prosperity to China.

1

This figure, carved in ivory, represents a public official. To obtain this job he had to take a series of very difficult exams.

2

Chinese doctors knew how to prepare medicines by boiling up herbs. They also treated patients by sticking needles in them (acupuncture).

3

Here is a scene from *The Water Margin*. This was one of China's few novels. It tells a story about bandits who protected the poor against wicked officials.

4

European missionaries, like these Jesuit priests were, at first, welcomed by the emperors, but later they were driven out.

5

Porcelain Silk
Jade Tea
Lacquer

Many people in Europe wanted to buy beautifully-made Chinese goods, like these. But Europeans had to pay in gold and silver because China did not want European goods.

Farming

In the countryside life continued with few changes. New crops, such as maize, were introduced from America by Spanish and Portuguese traders. During the period of peace under the Ch'ing emperors the population began to increase. At first this did not matter, but later, it became difficult to grow enough grain to feed everyone.

Life in Japan

The emperors of Japan were greatly honoured, but had no real power. The country was ruled by an official called the Shogun. The first Europeans reached Japan in the 1540s and for nearly a century they traded with the Japanese. But then the Shogun expelled all foreign merchants, except the Chinese and the Dutch, and the Japanese people remained totally cut off from the rest of the world until 1854.

In 1467, civil war broke out. For over 100 years, the local barons, called daimyos, fought each other. They built huge castles like this one, half-fortress, half-palace, where they lived with their warriors, the samurai. The samurai believed that the only honourable way of life was to fight for and give loyal service to their daimyo. Eventually, a powerful daimyo called Tokugawa Ieyasu, succeeded in uniting Japan. He became Shogun and ruled from his capital in Edo (now Tokyo). The Tokugawa family held power until 186

1 The ancient Japanese Shinto faith became popular again in the 18th century. Here a new baby is being brought to a Shinto shrine.

2 Tea drinking developed into an elaborate ceremony, which still plays an important part in Japanese life. Both the ceremony and the tea were originally brought from China by Buddhist monks. The way in which the tea is prepared, served and drunk follows strict rules.

3 Christianity was brought to Japan by Jesuits. They converted many people but later the Shoguns banned Christianity and had many Christians executed.

4 Arranging flowers was a special art, called Ikebana, which at first only men were allowed to do. The type of flowers and the way they are arranged have special meanings.

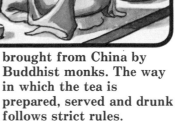

5 Pictures made by printing from carved blocks of wood became popular at this time. Most of them illustrate the lives of ordinary people.

6 This is a street bookseller in the early 18th century. Poetry and novels were still popular but there were no longer many women writers as there had been earlier.

7 Puppet theatres and a type of musical play called "Kabuki" became very popular. These were livelier and more realistic than older Japanese dramas.

A Dutch island

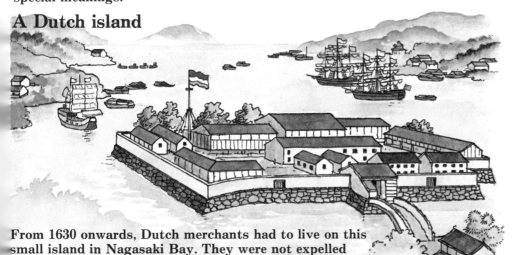

From 1630 onwards, Dutch merchants had to live on this small island in Nagasaki Bay. They were not expelled completely like other foreigners because the Shoguns felt they would not try to conquer or convert the Japanese. A bridge linked the island to the land, but the Dutch were not allowed to cross it.

Key dates

AD1467/1568	Period of civil war in Japan.
AD1543	First Portuguese traders reached Japan. Other Europeans follow.
AD1549/1551	**St Francis Xavier** working in Japan.
AD1592 & 1597	Japanese invaded Korea.
AD1600/1868	Tokugawa family rule.
AD1603	**Tokugawa Ieyasu** became Shogun.
AD1606/1630	Christians persecuted.
AD1623/1639	All Europeans, except a few Dutch, left Japan.

Merchants and Trade

Once explorers had discovered new lands and sea-routes in the 16th century, there was a huge increase in trade between Europe and the rest of the world. By the 17th century the main trading countries were Holland, England and France. In these countries the merchants and middle classes who organized this trade became very wealthy and began to copy the life-style of the nobles. Even some of the ordinary working people benefited from this increase in wealth.

Groups of merchants, like these, set up trading companies in which people could buy shares. The shareholders' money was used to pay the cost of trading ventures and any profit was divided amongst the shareholders.

Many merchants bought goods from people who worked in their own homes and sold them abroad. Here a merchant's agent is buying cloth from a family workshop.

Companies hired ships to export their goods. Countries competing for overseas trade had to have good ships, sailors and ports. Dutch ships were among the best in Europe.

Rich merchants began to band together to set up banks to lend money. For this service they charged a fee called "interest". People could also bring their money to the bank for safe-keeping. The first bankers were Italian merchants. In the 17th century London and Amsterdam became the most important banking cities.

In some of the big cities of Europe, coffee houses became the places where people met to buy and sell shares and discuss business.

It soon became more convenient to have a proper building for use as a market where people could buy and sell shares. This is the Amsterdam Stock Exchange, built in 1613. Soon there were stock exchanges like this in all the important trading centres of Europe.

Special insurance companies were set up. Merchants paid them a fee and if their trading expeditions met with disaster the insurance company stood the cost.

1 The new middle classes

As the merchant classes grew richer, they built themselves big town houses. The fashionable areas of big cities had pavements and wide streets.

2

The new middle classes wanted to live like the nobles. Many of them became rich enough to buy country estates and obtained titles. Some of the nobility looked down on them but others were happy to marry into these wealthy families.

3

Governments needed to understand business and finance so sometimes men from the merchant classes were chosen as royal ministers and advisers.

4

We know what many of the Dutch merchants of this time looked like because many of them paid artists to paint their portraits.

5

Many of the paintings of this time, especially Dutch ones, show us how merchant families lived and what their homes looked like.

6

In every country there were still many desperately poor people. Some nobles and merchants tried to help the poor. They founded hospitals, homes for old people and orphanages. Here a group of merchants' wives are inspecting an orphanage run by nuns.

Dutch merchants find Australia

On their trips to the east, Dutch sailors discovered Australia, which they called New Holland. Some people were wrecked there and tried to set up settlements but all their early attempts failed.

The Dutch controlled most of the important spice trade between Europe and the East Indies. This made Holland the greatest trading nation in Europe for much of the 17th century. This map shows the Dutch empire in the East Indies and the things they went there to buy.

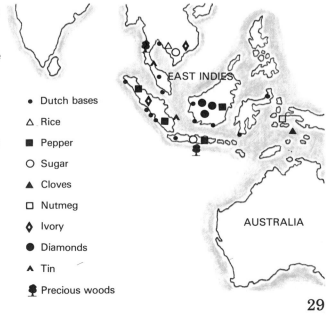

- • Dutch bases
- △ Rice
- ■ Pepper
- ○ Sugar
- ▲ Cloves
- □ Nutmeg
- ◆ Ivory
- ● Diamonds
- ▲ Tin
- ♣ Precious woods

Kings and Parliaments

In the 17th and 18th centuries much of Europe was ruled by kings, queens and emperors who were extremely powerful. These rulers are known as "absolute monarchs". The court of Louis XIV of France was the most brilliant in Europe. This is the Hall of Mirrors in his palace at Versailles. Louis encouraged the French nobles to come and live at his court, and spend their time in a round of entertainments, so that he could keep an eye on them. Other monarchs built themselves great palaces too and tried to imitate Louis' way of life.

1 The English parliament

Parliament supporter ("roundhead")

King's supporter ("cavalier")

King Charles I of England tried to ignore parliament and rule like an absolute monarch. Many people were so unhappy with the way he ruled that in 1642 civil war broke out.

The king was defeated and executed. Oliver Cromwell, the leader of the parliamentarian army became ruler. He could not get parliament to agree with him so he too tried to rule without parliament.

Oliver Cromwell died in 1658. His son was incompetent and no one would support his government. Eventually Charles I's son was invited back and crowned King Charles II.

2 Parliaments hardly ever met. The king took all the important decisions. His ministers could only advise him and carry out his instructions. In order to keep control a successful ruler, like Louis XIV, had to spend hours every day with his ministers in meetings like this one.

3 Sometimes the king's favourites became very powerful. Louis XV let Madame du Pompadour, shown above, make important decisions.

4 The king made the laws and could put his enemies in prison if he wanted. Law-courts did what the king wanted.

5 Absolute monarchs usually kept large, permanent armies. Frederick the Great of Prussia, which is now part of Germany, was a brilliant military commander. Here he is inspecting his troops.

6 Monarchs often brought great painters, musicians and writers to their courts. As a child, Mozart played the piano at the court of Maria Teresa.

7 To add to the strength of their countries rulers set up industries. Some of these produced luxury goods such as tapestries, silk and glass. This is a glassworks.

4 Parliament's power increased, however, and the king's minister had to have the support of its members. This is Robert Walpole one of the most successful ministers of the 18th century.

5 Members of parliament formed two political parties called the Whigs and the Tories. Only people who owned property worth more than a certain value could vote.

Key dates

AD1642	English Civil War began.
AD1643/1715	**Louis XIV** ruled France.
AD1649	**Charles I** was executed.
AD1658	**Oliver Cromwell** died.
AD1660/1685	Reign of **Charles II**.
AD1682/1725	**Peter the Great** ruled Russia.
AD1715/1774	**Louis XV** ruled France.
AD1730/1741	**Robert Walpole** was Prime Minister.
AD1740/1780	**Maria Teresa** ruled Austria.
AD1740/1786	**Frederick the Great** ruled Prussia (now part of Germany).
AD1756/1791	Life of **Mozart**.
AD1762/1796	**Catherine the Great** ruled Russia.

Index

Going Further

Books to read

If you look in a library or bookshop, you will find lots of books about this period of history. Here are a few of the interesting ones.

Everyday Life in Renaissance Times by E. R. Chamberlin (Carousel).
The Story of Britain in Tudor and Stuart Times by R. J. Unstead (Carousel).
Europe Finds the World, The Birth of Modern Europe, Martin Luther and *Benin*—4 books in the Cambridge Introduction to the History of Mankind (Cambridge University Press).
Cue for Treason by Geoffrey Trease (Puffin).
Popinjay Stairs by Geoffrey Trease (Puffin).
The Strangers by Anne Schlee (Puffin).
Jack Holborn by Leon Garfield (Puffin).

These books are novels.

Places to visit

There are lots of places where you can see things from this period of history. Most museums have furniture, costumes, weapons and everyday objects in their collections.

You can find out about museums all over Britain from a booklet called *Museums and Galleries* (British Leisure Publications), which you can buy in newsagents and bookshops.

Paintings can tell you a lot about this period too. They often show the clothes and houses of the people who had them painted. Look in art galleries and at art books in libraries.

Look out for great houses and houses once lived in by famous people. Some of these and other interesting historical places are listed in *History Around Us* by Nathaniel Harris (Hamlyn).